W9-BGZ-010

Purchased with

TITLE V

Grant funds

T 37754

ROLLING

RIGHT ALONG!

Annie Pitts, Burger Kid

Written and illustrated by

Diane deGroat

SeaStar Books
NEW YORK

Copyright © 2000 by Diane deGroat
First published in hardcover in 2000 by SeaStar Books, New York.

All rights reserved. No part of this book may be reproduced or utilized in any form or by any
means, electronic or mechanical, including photocopying, recording, or any information storage
and retrieval system, without permission in writing from the publisher.

SEASTAR BOOKS
a division of NORTH-SOUTH BOOKS INC.

First published in the United States by SeaStar Books, a division of North-South Books Inc.,
New York. Published simultaneously in Canada, Australia, and New Zealand by
North-South Books, an imprint of Nord-Süd Verlag AG, Gossau Zürich, Switzerland.

Library of Congress Cataloging-in-Publication Data
deGroat, Diane.
Annie Pitts, burger kid/by Diane deGroat
p. cm.
Summary: Third-grader Annie Pitts loves hamburgers and is
determined to become the Burger Barn's next poster child.
[1. Hamburgers—Fiction. 2. Thanksgiving Day—Fiction.
3. Contests—Fiction. 4. Humorous stories.] I. Title.
PZ7.D3639 Anf 2000
[Fic]—dc21   00-24304

The art for this book was prepared using pencil.
The text for this book is set in 13-point Palatino.

ISBN 1-58717-015-9 (trade binding)
1   3   5   7   9   TB   10   8   6   4   2
ISBN 1-58717-110-4 (paperback binding)
1   3   5   7   9   PB   10   8   6   4   2

Printed in the U.S.A.

For more information about our books, and the authors and artists who create them,
visit our web site: www.northsouth.com

Contents

✫　✫　✫

CHAPTER ONE

Ode to a Hamburger

Grease trickles from my lips,
Ketchup oozes, too.
I lick it from my fingertips . . .
Hamburger! I love you!

I did it! I had to write a poem for school and I couldn't think of anything to write about until we sat down at the Burger Barn Restaurant.

My teacher said to write about something we like. I was going to write about acting, which I really like, because I'm going to be a famous actress someday, but I couldn't think of anything to rhyme with "acting," except "subtracting."

Fortunately, I also like hamburgers, and when I bit into that double-double patty patty burger . . . Yes! A poem popped right into my head.

I repeated it to myself over and over so I wouldn't forget it. *"Grease trickles from my lips . . ."*

I needed to write it down. I grabbed a paper napkin, but I didn't have anything to write with.

"Ketchup oozes, too . . ."

I checked all my pockets. No pen.

"I lick it from my fingertips . . ."

I was about to start writing with the ketchup dispenser when I spotted Grandma coming back from the ladies' room.

I jumped up and shouted, "A pen! I need a pen quick!"

"Okay, okay," Grandma said as she slid into the booth. "I have one in here somewhere. . . ."

While she rummaged through her purse, I took another bite to help me remember the words.

"Hummerer! Ah wuv oo!" I said with my mouth full.

"Excuse me?" Grandma said, handing me the pen.

I chewed quickly, swallowed, then shouted, *"Hamburger! I love you!"* I grabbed the pen and wrote down all the words before I forgot them. Then I sat back and took a deep breath.

Grandma laughed. "Don't tell me. You had a sudden desire to write a love letter to your hamburger."

"It's my homework for tomorrow," I said. "We have to write a poem, and this hamburger inspired me."

I wasn't kidding. I love hamburgers. Grandma takes me to the Burger Barn whenever my mother has to work late. Sometimes Grandma would rather have pizza. Not me.

I could eat burgers every day and never get tired of them.

Grandma finished her turkey burger, the Thanksgiving Special, and pointed to the poster hanging on the wall. "That should be you on that poster, Annie," she said. "I don't know anyone who likes this place as much as you do."

I took a look at this month's Burger Barn poster. There was a big close-up of a little boy holding up a double-double patty-patty burger that was almost as big as he was.

As posters go, it was not very interesting, but someone had improved it by drawing a mustache on the kid. There were also some scars scratched all over his cheeks.

Each month there was a different "Burger Kid" on the poster. I don't know how they got chosen; they were just regular-looking kids. I thought about what Grandma said and I tried to picture myself on the poster.

"You're right," I agreed. "I would be a perfect model. After all, I love hamburgers, and I'm extremely *photogenic.*"

Photogenic was today's word on my Learn-a-Word-a-Day calendar. It means "suitable for posing." I'm certainly suitable for posing, because I practice every day in front of a mirror. So far I've perfected twelve different smiles that I can use when I become famous and have to get my picture taken a lot.

Grandma checked her watch and said, "My dear, you may be *photogenic,* but you're also up past your bedtime. Hurry up and finish."

"First look at this," I said. I gracefully picked up my half-eaten burger and pretended to model with it, just like the boy on the poster. I used Smile #1, my favorite. Four teeth showing on top, edges of mouth curled up ever so slightly, eyes twinkling.

When I saw my reflection in the window,

I looked just like a Burger Barn poster kid. Except that I had a big ketchup stain on the front of my shirt. I covered it with my right hand.

"How's this?" I said to Grandma out of the corner of my smile.

"You look like you're pledging allegiance to your hamburger," Grandma said.

"No, really," I said. "Wouldn't I make a good Burger Kid? How do you get to be on a poster?"

"I wouldn't know," Grandma said. "I've never been on one. And I don't think I'd want to, either. I wouldn't look good with a mustache."

"A mustache isn't so bad," I said, holding a strand of my curly red hair under my nose. "But I wouldn't want someone to draw snot coming out of my nose."

"Thank you for sharing that with me,"

Grandma said. "Now I'm really finished eating."

We got up to leave, and I stuffed the poem into my jacket pocket. I would have to remember to copy it onto notebook paper when I got home.

On the way out we passed Bob, the manager, putting up Thanksgiving decorations. I waved to him, but he didn't wave back. His hands were full of paper turkeys. Actually, he never waves back, but I'm sure he remembers me, because I'm here so often.

I stopped short at the poster by the door. There was a notice pasted across the top, saying:

> *Would your child like to be our next Burger Barn poster kid? Auditions are being held at the Cross County Shopping Center on November 24 at 10:00 A.M.*

Our photographers will be looking for that special someone, ages 2-15. Must be accompanied by an adult.

I couldn't believe it. Photographers were coming here to Yonkers to find a poster kid!

"Here's your chance," Grandma said, handing me my mittens. "November twenty-fourth is the day after Thanksgiving. There's no school, so we can stop by the mall if you want to audition."

Audition! That sounded so professional! I followed Grandma out the door, but not before ripping the notice off the poster and tossing it into the trash. I wouldn't want people wasting their time trying out for a contest that I was going to win.

As we walked to the bus stop Grandma said, "Now don't go making yourself crazy, Annie. A lot of people will be trying out, but

only one person gets picked for the poster. It might not be you."

That never even occurred to me. "Of course they'll pick me," I said. "I'm perfect for the poster. You said so yourself."

Grandma sighed. "I just don't want you to get your hopes up."

Well my hopes were about as up as they could get. They were up when we got on the bus. They were still up when we took off. Then right around Yonkers Avenue, I over-heard two ladies talking in the seat behind me.

One woman said, "My daughter is all excited about that poster contest. I'm having her hair done just for the audition. You know, she doesn't really eat those greasy hamburgers—they're bad for her skin—but she can *pretend* to eat it in front of the camera."

The other woman was not so sure. "But,

Marilyn," she said. "I thought they just wanted plain-looking people. Your Marsha might be too pretty for a hamburger ad."

Marsha! I knew that voice sounded familiar. The mother of Marsha-Miss-Teacher's-Pet was sitting right behind me, talking about the poster contest.

The last person I wanted to see on a poster was Marsha. She thinks she's so great. She probably even thinks that she could win the contest! I'll have a talk with her tomorrow. Because I, Annie Pitts, am going to be the next Burger Kid.

CHAPTER TWO

School Daze

Mom was already home when Grandma and I walked in.

I skipped into the kitchen, singing, "I'm going to be a Burger Kid . . ."

"Are you by any chance talking about that poster contest at the mall?" Mom asked.

"How did you know?"

She opened the paper to the community news page. A huge ad said: *Calling all kids! Come and get your picture taken. You may be on our next Burger Barn poster!*

"Oh, great," I said. "So now the whole world knows." I slid into the chair next to her and dropped my chin onto the table.

"It's not exactly a secret," she said. "Now, stop thinking about hamburgers for a minute and start thinking about turkey."

"Turkey?" I groaned.

"Yes, turkey," she said. "I'm working out the menu for Thanksgiving."

"What's to work out?" I groaned again. "Turkey, candied sweet potatoes, cranberry sauce, and some yucky vegetable. It's the same every year. And speaking of the same every year—is Mercedes coming?" Mercedes is my fourteen-year-old stuck-up cousin who lives in Connecticut and goes to a private school.

Mom said, "As a matter of fact, your aunt Lil called today. She and Mercedes would like to join us for the holiday as usual. Won't that be nice?" Mom had a fake smile on her face.

"Why do you always invite them anyway?" I asked. "Why can't it just be the three of us?"

Grandma said, "Here we go again. Thanksgiving is the only time I get to see my two daughters and my two granddaughters in the same place at the same time. I wish you'd all try to get along better."

Mom stared at the list she had been making and said, "I do try, Mom. It's Lil. She's such a fusspot. She criticizes everything I do."

"Mercedes doesn't even talk to me," I said. "She acts like I have cooties or something."

Grandma laughed. "We'll do a cootie-check tomorrow," she said. "But right now you have to get ready for bed. Scoot!"

When I got up the next morning, I tried not to think about how awful my Thanksgiving was going to be. I had other things to think about.

My word to learn for the day was *carnivorous*, meaning "meat eating," and I started thinking about a double-double patty-patty burger. I wouldn't mind having one for breakfast.

But Grandma had already made oatmeal. "None for me, thanks," I said as I sat at the table. "I'm *carnivorous.*"

Grandma laughed and said, "I suppose you'd like a hamburger for breakfast?"

"Why not?" I asked.

Grandma opened the bread drawer and took out a hamburger bun. She scooped a blob of oatmeal onto the bottom half, gracefully folded over the top half, and presented it to me with a bow.

Now, most people would think that oatmeal-on-a-bun would taste pretty awful, but I have to admit, with a little ketchup, it wasn't half bad. Next time I'll try it with lettuce and tomato, too.

Apparently I wasn't the only one thinking about hamburgers. When I got to school, everybody was talking about the poster contest. Even our teacher, Miss Goshengepfeffer. I know she likes the Burger Barn, because I've personally seen their wrappers in her trash can.

Miss G. *did* have an unusually big smile on her face when she called the class to order. It was the same kind of smile I have when I'm thinking about hamburgers.

So there we were, smiling and thinking about burgers, when Miss G. asked, "Now, who would like to go first?"

I thought she was talking about the poster contest, and since I wouldn't have minded being the first to get my picture taken, I raised my hand. So did Marsha-Miss-Me-First-Me-First.

Then I raised my hand higher than hers and called out, "Ooh, ooh," with a lot of smiling and waving because I wanted to show everyone just how serious I was about winning that contest—and to let Marsha know that she was up against some real competition.

Miss G. finally noticed me and said, "Annie, would you like to go first?"

"Yes, Miss G.," I answered.

"Well then, come up and read your poem."

I stared at her blankly.

Miss G. stared back and said, "Hello? You volunteered to be the first to read for us. You did write a poem, didn't you?"

I finally figured out that Miss G. was calling on people to present the poems that we had written last night. What I didn't quite figure out was how to tell her that my poem was written on a Burger Barn napkin and stuffed into my jacket pocket out in my locker. I had forgotten to copy it over.

"Uh . . . it's in my locker, Miss G.," I said.

"Somebody else can go first while I go get it." She nodded and called on Marsha-Miss-Hooray-I-Go-First, and I ran out to my locker.

When I got back to the room, Miss G. was saying, "That was lovely, Marsha. I especially enjoyed your very long description about the new dress that you got for Thanksgiving." Then she said, "Matthew, did I see your hand up?"

"I don't think so," he said. He checked to see just where his hands were. One was in his pocket, and the other was scratching his head. It was probably the scratching one that looked like it was volunteering.

"Well, how about sharing your poem with us anyway," Miss G. said.

Matthew groaned and walked to the front of the room. He held his paper in front of his face as he read:

Turkey is okay. . . . Stuffing is cool. . . .
But what I like about Thanksgiving is . . .
You don't have any school.

That had to be the worst poem I ever heard, but everyone else seemed to like it, even Miss G. As for Matthew, he was happy to be done with it. He raced back to his seat, which was, unfortunately, next to mine.

I waited until he noticed me glaring at him, and then I put my finger in my mouth and pretended to gag.

"Annie?" Miss G. said. "May we hear your poem now?"

I was in the middle of gagging, so I pretended to be coughing and clearing my throat. When I was all cleared up, I brought my Burger Barn napkin to the front of the room and carefully unfolded it.

It was a little hard to make out some of the

words through the grease stains, but the wonderful smell of last night's burger inspired me all over again. This was a poem you could read and smell at the same time! I read:

> *Grease trickles from my lips,*
> *Ketchup oozes, too.*
> *I lick it from my fingertips . . .*
> *Hamburger! I love you!*

And then I took a bow.

There was total silence until Matthew yelled, "That's the stupidest Thanksgiving poem I ever heard!"

And it was then that I remembered that the assignment was to tell what we liked about Thanksgiving, not about what we *like*. It was a small mistake, but I knew I was in big trouble. Miss G. has always said that I don't

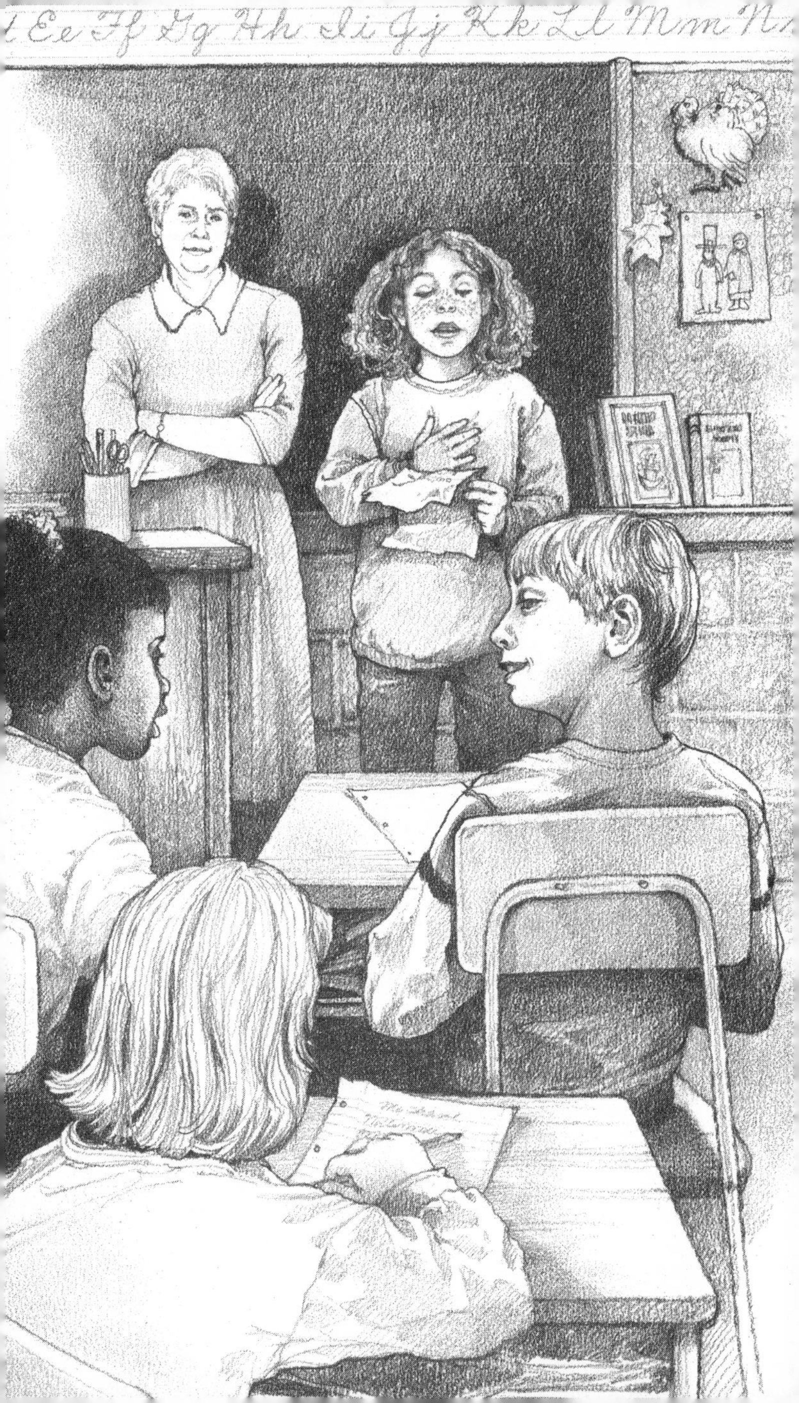
Ee Ff Gg Hh Ii Jj Kk Ll Mm

pay enough attention in class, and the next time that it happened, she would have to have a conference with my mother.

"Annie," Miss G. said sternly. "Was that your *Thanksgiving* poem?"

I knew my mother didn't have time to come in for a conference right now, what with my stuck-up relatives coming next week, so I answered, "Yes, Miss G. That's my Thanksgiving poem. We're having hamburgers for Thanksgiving. We're . . . *carnivorous.*"

Miss G. had a puzzled look on her face. Some kids giggled.

"That's fine, Annie," she said softly. "Not everyone can have turkey for Thanksgiving."

I took my seat, satisfied now that my mother would not have to come in for a conference. I scratched and sniffed my homework as I sat through the rest of the poems. Most of them were about turkey, of course.

Thomas's was interesting, though. He wrote a poem about going to a restaurant every Thanksgiving because his mother didn't want to cook. He said he always ordered the Turkey Special at Maxime's Restaurant.

I, Annie Pitts, would have ordered a hamburger.

Cootie Alert

On the night before Thanksgiving, I was hoping that Grandma could take me to the Burger Barn. I wanted to talk to my friend Bob, the manager, to see if he could give me any inside information about the poster contest. He might know what the photographers were looking for, and I thought he should share that information with me, because I was his best customer.

But Mom had other plans for us. Since

Aunt Lil called, my mother had become a cleaning tornado. She started by washing the kitchen curtains and, for the first time, I noticed that they were white, not tan. She even vacuumed behind the sofa where no one ever looks. But I guess Aunt Lil does.

And in the bathroom, Mom placed a pile of fancy paper "hand towels." When I asked what they were for, she said that some people prefer to use disposable paper towels instead of the regular cloth towels that are hanging in there. By "some people" she meant Aunt Lil, of course, and I was beginning to think that my aunt was one of those weirdos who thought that zillions of germs were out to get her.

I saw a man on TV once who wore a surgeon's gloves and mask all the time, and he wouldn't shake hands with anyone, because he was afraid of germs. The talk-show host brought in a hypnotist as a surprise to help the man overcome his fear. I don't know if it worked, but hiring a hypnotist for Aunt Lil would probably be easier than having to wipe out every germ in our house.

Just because Mom got into the whole cleaning thing, she expected Grandma and me to share in her enthusiasm. We helped, but Grandma finally put her foot down when Mom wanted her to remove her bowling trophies that decorated the windowsill. Grandma threw her hands in the air and said, "Lilian is your sister, for Pete's sake, not the queen of England! I think a house should look like people *live* in it!"

My room certainly looked like somebody lived in it, so Mom gave me a list of things to do, like put away my laundry. My laundry was freshly washed and very clean, so I would think that she would be proud to display it, but, no, she wanted it put away.

And then she wanted everything off the floor so we could vacuum. By "we" she meant "me," which I did. So after my aunt checks behind the living room sofa for dirt, she can check my floor for cooties—but she won't find any, because I, Annie Pitts, had VACUUMED!

When I finished I checked around for anything else besides cooties that might be *unsavory* to my relatives. *Unsavory* was my word to learn for Wednesday, and it meant "unpleasant."

I stared at the kitten calendar hanging on my wall and wondered if it might be *unsavory* to someone like Mercedes. I decided to leave it because it covered up a hole I accidentally made in the wall with my softball, and the hole would definitely be *unsavory* to my mother if she saw it.

The photo of the kitten sitting in a pile of autumn leaves was kind of cute, but the

calendar part was really dull. All of the squares were blank, except for November 23, which said "Thanksgiving."

Anyone who saw this might think that I was a really boring person, so I took a marker and started filling in the blank squares with things that a mature and exciting person should be doing in November.

The Friday after Thanksgiving was no problem. I wrote in "AUDITION." That left twenty-eight days to go.

In three of the squares I wrote "PARTY," and then I wrote "BIG PARTY" in three more squares. In preparation for all these parties, I filled in some of the blanks with "BUY HIGH HEELS" and "GET MANICURE."

To make it even more interesting, I wrote on Saturday, November 18, "GO ON DATE." I don't really date, but Mercedes probably does, so under "GO ON DATE," I wrote the

first name that popped into my head—
"WITH MATTHEW." The thought of actually going on a date with Matthew was
totally *unsavory,* but Mercedes wouldn't have
to know that. She would think that I led a
very mature and exciting life.

Now my room was ready for her visit. For
some reason I wanted her to like me. Even if
she is stuck-up, she's the only cousin that I
have. My father doesn't have any brothers or
sisters, so I don't have any cousins from his
side of the family.

I don't even see my father very often
because he lives in California. He said his
girlfriend, Tanya, is an actress. She hasn't
been in a movie yet, but she goes on a lot of
auditions. I hope I can meet her someday,
because we have so much in common, now
that I'm going on auditions, too.

Someday I'll visit them and meet all kinds

of movie stars doing their food shopping and stuff around the neighborhood just like regular people. Dad said he saw Oprah Winfrey once at a restaurant. He didn't get her autograph, though. He said it's not polite to ask a famous person for their autograph when they're doing personal things, like scarfing down lobster.

Well, after I win that poster contest, if somebody comes up to me and says, "Hey! Aren't you that famous Burger Kid?" I, Annie Pitts, will let them have my autograph. Even if it's Oprah herself.

CHAPTER FOUR

Another Turkey at the Table

On Thursday morning a storm ripped through the city with "freezing rain" and "gusting wind." That's how the weatherman described it, and I had to agree that it was pretty nasty. But that didn't stop the Macy's Thanksgiving Day parade.

I was glad because my own personal Thanksgiving tradition was watching the parade on TV while Mom and Grandma did the last-minute stuff for the big dinner. I helped by eating breakfast in front of the TV and by not getting in their way in the kitchen.

My favorite part of the parade is the floats. I could just picture myself on top of the Disney float, lipsynching the songs to *Pocohantas,* and waving to all the people waving at me. Maybe I'll be asked to do things like that after I become a Burger Kid.

I looked closely to see if I could recognize Pocohantas as a former Burger Kid. Suddenly, the giant Spiderman balloon came swooping out of nowhere, almost knocking Pocohantas off her float. With this wind, I wouldn't be surprised if Spiderman ended up here in Yonkers! The whole Northeast was stormy, and I was happy to be watching the parade from my warm and cozy living room with a nice hot breakfast—oatmeal-on-a-bun with ketchup, lettuce, and tomato.

I was singing along with Pocohantas, who

wasn't really singing—but I was—when my mother came in with tears in her eyes and a knife in her hand. She looked like something out of *The Revenge of the Killer Housewives.*

"Annie," she said, sobbing. "Could you please bring in the newspaper?" *Sob.* "It's getting soaked out there on the sidewalk." *Sniff.*

"You're crying about a wet newspaper?" I asked, relieved to hear that nobody was dead.

"Oh," *sob,* "I'm chopping onions for the stuffing," she explained. "That always makes me cry."

She went back into the kitchen to finish her chopping and her crying, and I went out to rescue a stupid newspaper from the rain. I mean—how much wetter could it get? But Mom looked so sad—even if it was just the onions—so I couldn't say no.

We live on the top floor of a two-family

house. So I stomped down the long flight of stairs to the front door. When I peeked out into the rain, I saw something weird on the stoop next to the sopping wet newspaper. It looked an awful lot like a turkey. Not a live turkey, but a plastic-wrapped supermarket turkey sitting right there on my stoop. Attached to it was an envelope that had "The Pitts Family" written on it.

It just so happened that my word to learn for today was *enigma.* It means "a puzzle or a mystery."And this was certainly an *enigma.*

I picked up the newspaper, and I tried to pick up the *enigma*, but it was too heavy. I tore off the envelope and brought that upstairs instead.

I stood in the doorway, so I wouldn't drip all over Mom's shiny clean floor before Aunt Lil got a chance to see it, and shouted, "Hey, there's a turkey outside on the steps."

"Anybody we know?" Grandma asked.

"I'm not kidding," I said, waving the wet envelope. "This was tied to it."

"That's strange," Grandma said, pulling a soggy card out of the envelope. "It says: 'Wishing you a happy Thanksgiving.' It's signed, 'Your PTA at P.S. 21.' It's from your school, Annie. Why would they send us a turkey?"

"It's an *enigma* to me," I said, practicing my new word. And then I suddenly realized something—"Or maybe it's because I told the class that we were having hamburgers for Thanksgiving."

Mom overheard me all the way from the kitchen and came in. "Why would you say something like that, Annie? You know we always have a turkey."

"It's a long story." I groaned. I didn't want to tell her I wasn't paying attention in class again, so I changed the subject. "What about that turkey down there? Should I try to bring it up?"

"We don't need two turkeys," Mom said. "We can give it to St. Paul's. The church kitchen is open today for the poor, and they'll be glad to have the extra food. But you'll have to take it over there this morning so that they can cook it."

I wasn't anxious to go out into the rain. All I wanted to do was sit and watch the parade like I did every Thanksgiving. But I didn't argue, because it was really my fault that there was a turkey out there in the first place.

I couldn't carry it all the way down the block by myself, so I got out my old doll stroller that was in the back of the closet.

I put on my raincoat and boots and went down the street, walking my fifteen-pound Butterball in the freezing rain and gusting wind, all the way to St. Paul's. I felt a little ridiculous, but I didn't think I was going to bump into anyone I knew strolling around in this weather.

The church was only a block away, but it took forever to get there, because garbage cans and tree limbs had blown all over the sidewalk. I left the turkey by the drop-off box and folded up the stroller. As I was leaving, I noticed some flashing lights and fire trucks on the next street, near where Matthew lives. Hmmm. Another *enigma*. I walked up the hill to see what was going on.

When I got close enough, I could see that a huge tree had blown over—and crashed right through the roof of Matthew's house! Matthew and his brother, Mark, were standing out on the sidewalk; their parents were talking to the police.

Matthew saw me coming and shouted through the rain, "Hey, Pitts! You should

have seen it! It was awesome! It missed me by an inch! My room is totaled!"

He was actually happy that an oak tree had almost killed him, and now here he was, standing outside in the rain in his pajamas.

I pulled my hood tighter as we watched the emergency repairmen unload a ladder from the truck. "What about all your stuff?" I asked.

Matthew was excited and said, "I can get all new stuff because the insurance is going to pay for it. Dad says I can even get a new skateboard. Isn't that cool?"

Before I could answer, Mrs. McGill ran over with an umbrella and said to Matthew, "You'd better come inside, sweetie. You'll catch cold out here." She looked very upset.

"Is there anything I can do?" I asked. I didn't really think there was, but people always say that when something bad happens, so I said it.

"We'll be okay," she answered. "A good part of the roof is damaged, and Matthew's room is a mess, but the rest of the house is okay. The worse part is having no electricity. The tree pulled down the wires. I can't even cook my turkey now." She looked at the hanging wires and sighed. "Some Thanksgiving," she said. "At least no one was hurt. I'm thankful for that."

I was going to ask Mrs. McGill if she wanted to use our oven, but I knew it wasn't big enough for two turkeys. They would probably go out for dinner. They could even get hamburgers if they wanted.

When I got to my house, Mom was waiting for me at the doorway. "What took you so long?" she asked. "I was getting worried."

I took off my wet coat and boots and dropped them out in the hallway. Then I explained about the tree and about Matthew almost getting killed. Mom got all upset and called up the McGills right away, saying things like "No, it's no bother," "really," and "I insist."

The next thing I heard was Mom saying, "I invited the McGills to join us for dinner. I thought they might as well have their Thanksgiving here, since it's such a disaster at their house. Mark and his father are helping with the repairs, so it'll probably be just Matthew and his mother. Could you put out two more plates, Annie?"

It took a while for all this to sink in, but then it hit me. "Matthew's coming here for Thanksgiving? At *my* house?" I plopped down onto the sofa and groaned. "Just what I need—another turkey at the table. Named Matthew."

"The McGills are our friends," Mom said sharply. "How would you feel if you were in Matthew's shoes?"

I certainly wouldn't want to be in Matthew's shoes—not because his room got totaled, but because he wears the oldest, smelliest sneakers I've ever seen. And then it occurred to me that maybe those old, smelly sneakers got destroyed in the crash, and Matthew would have to get new ones. But I bet he would miss the smelly ones because they were his favorites.

I felt sorry for Matthew, but I felt even sorrier for myself. Not only was I spending Thanksgiving with my stuck-up cousin, but I, Annie Pitts, was spending it with Matthew, too.

CHAPTER FIVE

Conversations with an Alien

We were planning to eat dinner about three o'clock, so I still had time to get used to the idea that Matthew would soon be sitting in my dining room, eating my food, and generally disturbing my peace.

Mercedes would be there, too, with her nose up in the air, trying hard not to get cooties from me, or whatever it is she thinks I have.

It would be great if the two of them could

just annoy each other, and leave me out of it altogether. Then I could eat my dinner in peace and quiet.

I set out two more places at the table and brought a chair in from the kitchen. Mom and Grandma usually sit on the ends. If Mercedes and Matthew could sit together on one side of the table, I wouldn't have to talk to either of them. But that left me on the other side with Aunt Lil and Mrs. McGill.

I figured I could handle that as long as Aunt Lil didn't keep saying that I should get my hair cut or straightened or tied back so it doesn't keep flying all over the place. She really had this thing about neatness, and it could make a kid nervous after a while.

I took a shower and washed my hair. I even cleaned under my fingernails to get out all the pumpkin pie batter that had gotten in there while I was licking the bowl. Of course

I wouldn't mind having a pumpkin-flavored finger to suck on all day, but Aunt Lil probably wouldn't appreciate it.

I got dressed in very clean underwear, socks that had stains only on the bottoms where nobody could see, and, finally, to top it off, the ugliest dress in the world. I even had a name for it—Ugly Dress. It was a hand-me-down from Cousin Mercedes—a long dress with little blue flowers all over it and a big, stupid bow in the back. It looked like something the *Little House on the Prairie* girl would wear when she went prancing through the meadow. I figured Aunt Lil couldn't say anything bad about it because she was the one who actually bought it for her kid.

The doorbell rang at 2:30. It was either Matthew or Mercedes, and, fortunately, I only had to put up with whoever it was until the other one came. Then, if my plan worked, the two of them could start annoying each other on their side of the table and leave me alone.

Mrs. McGill appeared at the door with bags of food and a short person in a gray suit.

"Hello, everybody," she said. "Thank you so much for sharing your turkey with us. I brought some dessert. Matthew, where are your manners?"

The short person she called Matthew didn't open his mouth, but I heard a "Hello" mumble out of it. Who was this person? And where was Matthew? It was another *enigma.*

Upon closer inspection, I decided there could be only one explanation. This was Matthew's body, taken over by well-dressed aliens.

And it was obvious that Mrs. McGill had fallen right into their trap. She thought that this short person in the gray suit was her son.

Mom thought so, too, and said, "Matthew, don't you look nice!"

The alien grunted something and it sounded an awful lot like the way Matthew grunts when he's mad about something.

"All of Matthew's clothes were soaked from the storm," Mrs. McGill explained. "But his good suit was protected by the dry-cleaner's bag. Doesn't he look wonderful all dressed up?"

Mom and Grandma agreed that the gray suit was just wonderful. Then the ladies brought the bags into the kitchen and I was left alone with the gray-suited alien. I leaned forward to see if I could spot any antennae when it suddenly mumbled, "You said you were having hamburgers."

I jumped back. It sure sounded like Matthew. I stuck my face close to his. "Who's in there?" I asked.

It answered, "Bug off, Slimebreath." Only Matthew calls me Slimebreath, so this had to be him after all.

So there we were, the two of us, standing around in our stupid clothes, trying not to look at each other. I'm sure my mother wouldn't want Matthew and me calling each other names like "Slimebreath," so I had to think of something else to say.

"Would you like some cider?" I asked as politely as I could.

"Apple cider?" he asked.

"Of course," I said. "What other kind is there?"

"I don't know. But I don't like apple cider."

"We have soda," I offered.

"Orange?"

"No. Cola."

"Diet?"

"I think so."

"I don't like diet soda."

"What about milk?"

"What about it?"

"Do you like it?"

"It's okay."

"Do you want some?"

"No."

"Do you want anything?"

"No."

"Fine."

"Fine."

I thought this polite conversation was going pretty well, so I continued. "So, Matthew," I said. "Are you trying out for the poster contest tomorrow? Everyone else seems to be."

"No way," he answered. "I don't want my picture on a stupid poster so people could draw pimples all over it."

"Well, I do," I said. "Besides, you get a free hamburger if you try out."

"Says who?"

"Says nobody. But they take your picture with one, so you probably get to eat it."

To that Matthew said, "Well, what if everybody uses the same hamburger and they get their spit all over it?"

"They wouldn't do that," I said, but I wasn't really sure. I stood there thinking about whether I would put my mouth on a hamburger that two hundred other people had already put their mouths on, while Matthew looked around the dining room.

"Who else is coming?" he asked.

"My aunt Lil and my cousin, Mercedes."

"You have a cousin named after a car?"

"I think she was named after a Roman goddess."

"I was named after a saint," Matthew said.

"Which one?"

"Saint Matthew, stupid!"

I could see that this polite conversation had taken a turn for the worse, and I wished Mercedes-the-Roman-goddess would hurry up and get here.

As if on cue, the doorbell rang. "Finally," I said, a little too loudly to be polite. I pressed the door buzzer to let them in. Grandma heard the bell and came into the living room, and we all stood around the doorway waiting for the last of our guests to come up the stairs. Aunt Lil came in first. "I'm so sorry we're late, Mother. We had a *dreadful* time driving through this *dreadful* weather!"

Grandma laughed. "Well, we're *dreadfully* glad that you made it. We were getting worried." She hugged Aunt Lil, then said, "And where's my darling granddaughter?"

A girl appeared in the doorway. She had Mercedes's face, but unlike my cousin, she wore really sloppy clothes—torn jeans, a floppy hat, an old army coat . . . and a nose ring.

Okay. So maybe Matthew's body wasn't really taken over by aliens, but I'm sure they got Mercedes! Was I the only one who noticed these things?

Aunt Lil gave a heavy sigh, looked at the ceiling, and with a freshly manicured hand, she lifted the floppy hat. And that's when we saw IT. Not only did the aliens dress my cousin in messy clothes and put a ring in her nose, but they shaved her head.

I, Annie Pitts, had a bald cousin.

CHAPTER SIX

Let's Talk Turkey

So there we were, staring at my bald cousin with the ring in her nose and a grin on her face. She was obviously enjoying everybody's reaction.

"She's going through a phase . . . ," Aunt Lil explained. Actually, Mercedes looked like she had been through a lawn mower.

But Grandma gave her a hug anyway and said, "I think it looks great, honey. Sometimes we need a change from the ordinary." This, of course, was coming from a woman who dyes her hair neon orange.

I was about to give my opinion on what I thought of bald teenagers when Aunt Lil interrupted. "Oh, before I forget—there's a turkey downstairs in the hallway."

"A turkey?" Mom and Grandma said in unison.

"Yes—it's all wrapped up in lovely pink plastic. Did you order from the gourmet shop like I suggested? I know how hard it is to make a really moist turkey. . . ."

"I'll go take a look," Grandma said. Of course she was looking at me when she said it.

Meanwhile, Matthew had been staring at Mercedes ever since she walked through the door.

He said, "You look like that lady from the *Star Trek* movie. You know—the one from that weird planet."

Matthew didn't disappoint me. He said the stupidest thing he could have said to Mercedes-the-Bald.

I expected her to tell Matthew to bug off, but instead she said, "You like *Star Trek*, too? I've seen every movie and every TV show a zillion times."

"Me, too!" Matthew said.

Okay—they weren't exactly annoying each other yet, but there was still time.

Grandma appeared at the door with a fully cooked, pink plastic-wrapped turkey. "Compliments of Miss Goshengepfeffer," she announced, holding up a card. "Apparently, your teacher feels that no one should have to eat hamburgers for Thanksgiving, Annie."

I groaned. "So what's wrong with hamburgers?" I said to no one in particular. "Is it some kind of law that you have to have a turkey on Thanksgiving? I'd rather have a hamburger!"

"I wouldn't," Mercedes said. "I don't even want turkey. I'm a vegetarian."

This was Matthew's chance to say something really stupid, like eating too many vegetables can make your hair fall out. But he listened politely as Mercedes explained how she doesn't believe in eating anything that has a face.

This was getting weird.

"Dinner's ready," Mom called.

I was ready for Plan B. I rushed into the dining room first.

"I'll sit here," I said, grabbing the middle chair on my side of the table. "Matthew and Mercedes can sit over there." I pointed to the two chairs opposite me and everyone sat down.

The dinner started off quite peacefully. There was the usual Thanksgiving conversation.

"Everything looks *so* delicious."

"Does everyone have drinks?"

Of course, I politely joined the conversation. "I made the pumpkin pie," I said proudly.

"Nobody really likes pumpkin pie," said Matthew-the-Kid-Who-Knows-Everything. "You only made it because you're supposed to on Thanksgiving. Like turkey."

I wanted to say something back, but Mom was looking right at me, giving me her Don't-Even-Think-About-It look. I started eating instead. I started on my plateful of turkey when I felt something in my hair. Aunt Lil was petting my head like I was a poodle or something.

"Such beautiful red hair." She sighed. "Mercedes used to have beautiful red hair. . . ."

"Uh, it'll grow back," I said, pulling my head away from her hand.

"Yes. Someday. . . ." she said, looking off into space.

"Dark or white?" Mrs. McGill said, poking me with a platter full of turkey.

"Uh—no thanks," I answered. "I still have some."

"Have more," she said, dumping another helping onto my plate. I didn't stop her because I was busy trying to catch some of the conversation between Matthew and Mercedes.

"I don't really look like this," Matthew explained. "A tree fell on my house and all my clothes got wet. Except for this suit. Do you have to shave your head every day?"

Good, I thought. Matthew was making a pest of himself.

But Mercedes didn't seem annoyed. She said, "Sometimes I let it grow in for a week. Then it gets all fuzzy. Did a tree really fall on your house?"

I felt something on my shoulder. Aunt Lil

was rubbing my sleeve. "I remember this dress," she said sadly. "Mercedes looked lovely in it. . . ."

I was scarfing down more turkey, still trying to hear across the table. "Can I feel it?" Matthew asked. I couldn't believe he wanted to touch a bald head.

"Sure," Mercedes said. "Everybody wants to."

"There's some whiskers over here."

"I guess I missed a spot this morning."

Aunt Lil was still babbling. "She wore this dress on her ninth birthday. All the girls wore white gloves to the party. Did I give you the gloves with the dress, Annie?"

"Um—I don't remember," I said, staring at Matthew and Mercedes. They were having a very nice conversation. It was a little on the gross side—I mean—talking about my cousin's whiskers and all. But they seemed to be having a good time.

"What happens when you have to blow your nose?" Matthew asked with great interest. "Do the boogers get all over the earring— I mean nose ring?"

"No. It's not really in the way."

"Who wants more turkey?" Grandma said, bringing in another platter. "Matthew?"

Matthew didn't answer. He was staring up close and personal at Mercedes's nose ring. "Did it hurt when you got it pierced?"

"A little. They spray some stuff on to numb it first. You should get an earring, Matthew. It looks cool on guys."

"Annie needs some more turkey over here," Mrs. McGill said when the platter came around again. I was so busy listening that I didn't realize I was stuffing myself with everything Mrs. McGill put on my plate. I think I had four helpings of turkey, but I lost count.

"Mercedes used to eat turkey," Aunt Lil said. "She used to have a full head of hair, too. Just like yours, Annie. But she wore it up like this."

She grabbed a handful of my hair and pulled it back with a jerk. The fork, which was about to enter my mouth, flew forward and a glob of cranberry sauce landed on Matthew's newly dry-cleaned jacket. To my surprise, he didn't even notice the wet little blob that was stuck to his lapel. He just kept right on talking.

I don't think Matthew has ever said that many sentences to me in my whole life. But to Mercedes he said things like, "Did you ever see the *Star Trek* episode with the Tribbles? It was my favorite."

Of course she answered, "Mine, too. . . ."

Mrs. McGill interrupted my staring and said, "You're such a good eater, Annie.

With Matthew, it's just pick, pick, pick. Even when he was a baby, he would just pick, pick, pick. . . ."

I really didn't want to hear about Matthew's personal eating habits. What I wanted was to be part of what was happening on the other side of the table. Mercedes was being really nice, so was Matthew. Why wouldn't they talk to me, too? I was feeling left out. I decided I would just have to join the conversation myself. I could try out some of the new words that I had memorized from my Learn-a-Word-a-Day calendar. That would surely impress them.

"So, Mercedes," I said loudly. "How long have you been un-*carnivorous*?"

She chuckled and answered, "I've been a vegetarian for almost a year now. I don't eat meat or poultry, but sometimes I do eat fish." She looked at my fully loaded plate and added, "But I see that you are quite a carnivore yourself!"

"Well," I said. "It's an *enigma* to me how somebody couldn't like hamburgers. I don't find them *unsavory* at all. In fact, I plan to be on a Burger Barn poster. I'm going to audition tomorrow, because I am so *photogenic*."

Before she could respond to my impressive statement, Matthew barged in. "I think *you* should try out for the poster, Mercedes. They might want to use an interesting-looking person like you."

Mercedes smiled and said, "I don't want to be in a hamburger ad, Matthew. I'm a vegetarian! But you should do it. You have an interesting face."

Matthew blushed and I just about gagged. Then Mrs. McGill said, "I told Matthew he should try out because he's so handsome. But he didn't want to."

"Maybe I will," he said.

That was the last straw. I blurted out, "Well, if you do audition, you'd better go after me, because you'll break the camera with that ugly thing you call a face."

"Annie!" my mother said sternly. "Matthew is a guest in our home."

"I was making conversation," I said. I suppose I could have said something more polite, but I was mad at Matthew. I just wasn't sure why.

I thought about heaving another spoonful of cranberry sauce in Matthew's direction, but my mother would probably notice something like that and say I was doing it on purpose. Even if I was.

The best way to do it would be to start with something small—say a pea. Yes, a petite pea flung by a fork could go a long way. In fact, it could go right up Matthew's nostril, if I aimed just right.

I carefully placed one small pea on the end

of my fork, checked to make sure my mother wasn't looking, and gave it a snap. The pea didn't go anywhere, but my fork slammed against my glass of cider, and the cider spilled into my lap. All over Ugly Dress.

Matthew burst out laughing.

Aunt Lil burst out crying.

Things were going from bad to worse.

CHAPTER SEVEN

Let's <u>Not</u> Talk Turkey

I ran to my room and slammed the door. I dropped Ugly Dress on the floor and stood in front of the closet trying to figure out what to wear. Should I get dressed up like Matthew, or should I put on sloppy clothes like Mercedes? I didn't really care.

Someone knocked on the door. "Annie, can I come in?" It was Grandma.

I opened the door a crack and she slid in. "Are you okay?" she asked.

"I'm okay," I said. "But that stupid dress is a wreck. Actually that's the best thing that happened to me today." I kicked Ugly Dress into the back corner of my closet. Then I said, "I suppose now I'm going to get Mercedes's ripped-up pants when she outgrows them. Why is she wearing that outfit anyway? And why is she being so nice to Matthew?"

"Because Matthew is nice to her," Grandma said.

"He hates me," I said. "And I don't like him, either."

Grandma meanwhile noticed my kitten calendar. She pointed to November 18. "Hmmm," she said. "It looks like you had a date with Matthew—does that say Matthew—last Saturday. Did you like him then?"

I forgot about the calendar. "Of course not," I answered. I picked up the marker and scribbled all over the November 18 square.

"I wrote that just so Mercedes would think I was an interesting person. I wanted her to like me."

"What makes you think she doesn't like you?" Grandma asked. "All you had to do was be a little nicer to Matthew and things would have been fine."

"Why should I be nice to him? He's always bothering me in school."

"That means he likes you," she said. "Otherwise he wouldn't bother with you at all."

I changed the subject and asked, "Do you really like Mercedes's bald head? I think it's gross."

Grandma pulled out some jeans from my dresser drawer and handed them to me. "It's just your cousin's way of expressing herself. Some people shave their heads; others fling peas across the table."

"I was aiming for Matthew's nostril," I explained. "I missed." I put on the jeans and a sweater that Grandma picked out for me, but I wasn't anxious to get back to dinner. I was so full that I even had trouble zipping my pants, but Grandma said she could use some dessert.

I looked at myself in the mirror. Except for my hair, I looked pretty ordinary. Tomorrow, I'd have to fix myself up somehow. I asked Grandma, "What do you think I should wear for the audition tomorrow? I want to get the judges' attention."

"Maybe you could shave your head." Grandma said, half joking. She stood behind me in the mirror and pulled my hair off my face to see how I'd look.

I made a face. "I don't think so," I said.

She laughed and said, "How about a nose ring?"

I groaned.

"Just a minute," Grandma said. She went to her room and came back with a folded sheet of paper.

"What's that?" I asked.

She waved the paper with a flourish and said, "You want to get attention? How about a tattoo?"

"You've got to be kidding," I said. "What are you doing with tattoos?"

"It's another one of my garage sale treasures," she said, opening up the sheet. "It's okay. They're temporary. Here, pick one."

I looked over the tattoos—there were some roses, a skull, several dragons, butterflies, a Tasmanian devil, and a cow.

"Are you sure they come off?"

"Positive."

I picked the cow because it looked a lot like the cow that the Burger Barn uses in its ad.

We walked across the hall to the bathroom and Grandma wet one of the disposable paper towels that my mother put out for Aunt Lil, so she wouldn't have to touch our regular ones.

"Where do you want it?" she asked.

"How about right here?" I pointed to my cheek.

She placed the tattoo on my cheek, then dabbed it with the wet towel.

When it was all soaked, she pulled off the backing and said, "Ta-da! You have a cow on your face. That'll get their attention."

It certainly got my mother's attention when we walked back into the dining room. "A tattoo! Annie! Mother! What have you done!"

"You never said I couldn't get a tattoo," I said, surprised at her reaction. "You said I couldn't get my ears pierced or wear fake

fingernails. You never mentioned anything about a tattoo."

Meanwhile, Matthew was stuffing his face with Grandma's apple pie, the chocolate cake that Aunt Lil had brought, and some chocolate pecan pie that his mother had picked up at the bakery. I noticed that he didn't touch any of the pumpkin pie that I had made.

I sat down, but I didn't want any dessert. I didn't even want to look at food anymore. I had eaten so much turkey, it felt like the whole fifteen-pound Butterball was just lying there in my stomach.

Grandma was busy explaining to Mom that the tattoo was removable, while I was busy holding my stomach.

Mrs. McGill turned to me and asked, "Are you okay, Annie?" I noticed she was eating my pumpkin pie, but that didn't make me feel any better.

"She looks a little green," Aunt Lil said, feeling my forehead.

Mom stopped her tattoo discussion long enough to give me her Are-You-Going-to-Embarrass-Me look. She said, "Do you have a problem, Annie?"

"I don't feel so good," I said weakly.

"Are you gonna barf?" Matthew-the-Pumpkin-Pie-Hater asked loudly.

"No," I said weakly. Then I changed my mind.

I made it to the bathroom just in time, but I swore that I, Annie Pitts, would never, ever, eat turkey again.

CHAPTER EIGHT

(Not) Little Orphan Annie

By Friday morning the rain had stopped and I was feeling much better. But every time I thought about that turkey, I felt a little queasy. At my request Mom had hidden any leftovers in the back of the refrigerator. She didn't even make her famous turkey soup like she usually does the day after Thanksgiving. The smell alone would've killed me.

When I came into the kitchen, Mom was on the phone and Grandma was fixing me breakfast—oatmeal-on-a-bun.

"Good morning," Grandma said. "Feeling better?"

"A little. Is my cow still on?"

"Still there."

"Good," I said, taking a small bite of the bun. "I want it to show when I get my picture taken."

Mom hung up the phone and said, "Matthew's going with you and Grandma to the mall this morning."

"Excuse me?" I said. Maybe I hadn't heard her right.

Mom explained, "Mrs. McGill is trying to clean out Matthew's room, and Matthew's whining and carrying on because he doesn't want her to throw anything out. She'd like him out of the house, so I told her to send him over here. You don't mind if he tags along with you, do you, Annie?"

"Yes, I do," I said grumpily.

Grandma raised her eyebrows at me. It

was her Try-to-Be-Nice-to-Matthew look. Anyway, it wasn't as if he had a chance to win the contest or anything. Let him come, I thought.

I got dressed and checked my Learn-a-Word-a-Day calendar. My word to learn for today was *moniker,* meaning "name." I tried it out. "My *moniker* is Annie Pitts. Matthew's *moniker* is Creepface."

Creepface showed up a few minutes later in his regular clothes—jeans, a sweatshirt, and his smelly old sneakers. I noticed that they were a little soggy. I also noticed that his eyes were red like he'd been crying.

I didn't have to talk to him much, because Grandma hurried us out the door to catch the bus. Matthew just sat and grumped the whole ride, mumbling things like, "She's probably throwing out my baseball card collection right now."

And I helped by saying reassuring things like, "Yeah, probably."

When we got to the Cross County Shopping Center, we saw some TV trucks in the parking lot. "Look!" I said. "We're going to be on the news!"

"Not if we can't get through that crowd," Grandma said.

We followed her toward the Burger Barn, but we couldn't get near it because of the mob of kids and parents. A policeman directed us to the end of a line that was almost as long as the mall itself.

"I can't believe all these kids want to be on a poster!" Matthew said. "What's the big deal?"

A boy in line in front of us turned around and said, "The big deal is the free hamburger coupons they give you just for getting your picture taken—ten of them!"

"*All right!*" Matthew said.

So that was it. Free hamburgers. This was a line full of some very *carnivorous* people, not necessarily *photogenic* people. I felt a little better.

I spotted Susan, one of my classmates, coming out of the Burger Barn. When she reached us, she showed us her coupons.

"It's fun," she said. "They give you a burger and then they take your picture."

"Is that it?" I asked.

Susan stuffed the coupons into her mother's purse and said, "First you have to fill out a bunch of papers. And then someone interviews you."

Matthew didn't look happy about that and said, "What do they ask you?"

"Well, they ask you if you like Burger Barn burgers, and you have to say, 'I love Burger Barn burgers' real loud. Then they write stuff down and take your picture."

"That sounds simple enough," Grandma said.

I agreed, but just in case, I repeated over and over to myself, "I love Burger Barn burgers, I *love* Burger Barn burgers, I love *Burger Barn* burgers . . ."

The line finally moved up to the Burger Barn entrance, and I was beginning to get a little nervous. I hadn't prepared a speech or anything, in case they wanted to interview the winner.

Bob, the manager, was at the door letting in a few people at a time.

"You go first," I said to Matthew. "I want to see what they make you do."

When we entered the restaurant, Grandma signed forms for Matthew and then for me at a table that was set up near the door. Then we moved on to table #2, where a grouchy lady asked Matthew some questions.

"Weight?"

Matthew shrugged. "I don't know."

"He's about fifty pounds," Grandma said. "Same as my granddaughter here."

The lady wrote "50," then said, "Height?"

Matthew looked at Grandma. Grandma guessed, "Four feet."

"Eyes?"

Matthew finally had an answer. "Two."

"Two what?"

"Two eyes."

"And what color might those two eyes be?" The lady squinted and took a look for herself. She wrote "brown."

"Hair?"

"Yes."

She wrote "blond."

"Next!"

I certainly wouldn't need any help. I stood up straight and said, "My *moniker* is Annie Pitts. I'm forty-seven inches tall, and I weighed fifty-two pounds at my last check-up. But that was after eating a few of those DELICIOUS BURGER BARN BURGERS!" I said it real loud in case any of the judges were around.

I continued, "My eyes are blue with little specks of brown, and my hair is an autumn shade of crimson."

The woman wrote down "redhead" and said, "Just like Little Orphan Annie."

I froze. I hate it when someone says I look like Little Orphan Annie. People have been calling me that ever since I was a baby. Strangers would come up to my mother in the supermarket and say, "Now doesn't she look like Little Orphan Annie!"

Then they would ask me, "And what's your name, little girl?" And when I said "Annie," they thought that was the most hysterical thing they'd ever heard.

"Next!"

I guess that meant we were all done with table #2, and so we moved on. The man behind table #3 had on a bright plaid jacket and a red bow tie. His name tag said *Sam* and I could tell he would appreciate real talent when he saw it.

He nodded to Matthew and Matthew mumbled, "I love Burger Barn burgers" with all the enthusiasm of a dead fish.

When it was my turn, I smiled one of those smiles I had been practicing—#3—with no teeth showing. Then I turned my tattooed cheek out and shouted, "I LOVE BURGER BARN BURGERS—ESPECIALLY THE DOUBLE-DOUBLE PATTY-PATTY BURGER!" I flung my arms out and I, Annie Pitts, smacked my grandma in the face.

CHAPTER NINE

Lights!
Camera!
Chomp!

I'm fine, I'm fine," Grandma said, holding her lip. Thank goodness she didn't make a big deal out of me smacking her, and the interview continued.

"That's quite a performance," Sam said.

Grandma dabbed her lip with a tissue and said, "That's no performance. She really does love hamburgers."

Sam wrote something in his notes, then said, "You know who you look like?"

I took a wild guess and said, "Little Orphan Annie?"

"Yeah," he said. "Now tell me . . ." He looked at the top of my form. "Tell me . . . Annie . . . your name is Annie? I'll be darned. Tell me, Annie. Why do you want to be a Burger Kid?"

I clenched my teeth and smiled. It was like the Miss America contest where they ask a contestant one question and she has to come up with a really smart answer or she'll never win.

So I said the first thing that came to mind:

> *Grease trickles from my lips,*
> *Ketchup oozes, too.*
> *I lick it from my fingertips . . .*
> *Hamburger! I love you!*

Then I bowed.

Sam stared at me, long after I was done bowing, probably because he had never seen such an impressive performance.

I stood with my frozen smile while he finally wrote some more stuff in his notes.

This is going great, I thought.

We were moved along to table #4 where a woman handed me a burger all wrapped up, and I could feel that it was still warm. It occurred to me that I hadn't had a hamburger in almost two weeks. I practically drooled just thinking about it.

The burger lady then sent me to the photographer where Matthew was just finishing up. One of the restaurant booths was all lit up with special lights and cameras. I felt like a famous person already!

I also felt a little queasy just thinking about how important that first bite was going to be.

The photographer said, "Okay, kid. Here's

what you do. You sit in the booth. You take a big bite. Then you give me your best smile. Let's go."

I slid into the booth and smiled my Smile #1 into the camera. "How's this?" I asked. I wanted it to be perfect.

"Fine," he said. "Now take a bite."

I unwrapped the steaming burger and that's when I smelled IT. That *unsavory* smell I had been avoiding since yesterday. I could have sworn it was TURKEY.

"What's this?" I shouted, staring at the bun in my hands.

"It's a turkey burger," the photographer said impatiently. "Is there a problem?"

"I thought it was a hamburger!"

"Hamburger, turkey burger. What's the difference? Do you want your picture taken or not?"

My stomach said no, but my mouth opened

wide. I bit off a chunk, but I didn't chew it or swallow. While the photographer was fumbling with the camera, it took all of my acting skills just to pretend that I was enjoying having this unchewed wad of turkey in my mouth. The seconds grew longer and longer. I could feel the sweat forming on my forehead. I kept smiling, even though the smell and the taste of the turkey burger was making me nauseous.

Flash! The camera clicked. It was over. "Next!"

I looked for the wrapper so I could spit out the unchewed turkey, but the assistant had removed it already.

I got up from the booth and almost knocked over the next kid in line as I hurried for the door, looking for someplace to spit. I stepped outside, hoping to find a trash can, when suddenly a microphone was stuck in my face.

A reporter shouted, "Hey, kid! Do you think you'll win the contest?" A cameraman was right behind him.

Of course I couldn't answer. My mouth was full of turkey burger.

"Don't be nervous," he said. "It's only national TV with eight million people watching!"

Eight million people? I coughed and the wad of turkey burger flew out, right in front of the camera. The reporter quickly turned his microphone on to someone else, in case there was more turkey hurling, but that was it.

"Nice going, Pitts!" Matthew said. He was standing right behind me. "Or should I call you 'Spitts'?"

"It was TURKEY!" I said suddenly, now that my mouth was empty. "If I don't win that contest, it's because of that stupid TURKEY!"

"Forget about it," Matthew said. "You're not going to win because you *are* a turkey." I was about to tell him what *he* was, but Grandma grabbed us each by the shoulder and led us back to the bus stop.

By Monday, I was still going over the audition in my mind. I tried to forget about the reporter getting spit on, but Matthew didn't. He told everyone in school how I grossed him out at the mall.

Fortunately, it didn't show up on the six o'clock news. I guess they figured it wasn't something people wanted to see at dinnertime.

But I missed my chance to be on TV. If I didn't have a mouthful of turkey, I could have been properly interviewed. And when the reporter asked if I thought I was going to win the contest, I could have answered, "Yes! I, Annie Pitts, will be the next Burger Kid!"

CHAPTER TEN

And the Winner Is . . .

Two weeks after Thanksgiving, Grandma and I headed for the Burger Barn. The new poster was supposed to be up, and we'd finally see who won the contest. I brought my free coupons, but I wasn't really hungry. I was too excited.

I ran from the bus stop, dragging Grandma along with me.

"Please, Annie . . . ," she kept saying. "I know how much you want to win, but you may be disappointed if . . ."

I didn't want to hear it. I only remembered how much I impressed Sam, the talent agent.

But when we reached the Burger Barn, the old poster was still up! The little kid with the mustache and the scars—and now some blacked-out teeth—was still smiling back at us.

"Where's the new one!" I shouted.

"I guess they didn't put it up yet," Grandma said. "Let's go inside and ask."

I spotted Bob, taking down the Thanksgiving decorations and putting up Santa Clauses. I ran across the room, waving my arms and shouting, "Where's the new poster! Who won! Was it me?"

Bob looked down from the top of the ladder and said, "Take it easy, kid. I just got them in today. When I finish here I'll get them from the back room. You're not the only one who wants to know."

It was then that I looked around and noticed the larger-than-usual crowd at the

Burger Barn. Even Marsha-Miss-I-Never-Eat-Hamburgers was there with her mother.

When Bob finally brought the package out, the eager crowd formed a circle around him. We leaned in close as he cut the tape with a knife. I held my breath.

He pulled back the cardboard flaps, and there they were—a stack of posters all shiny and new.

And totally blank.

"I guess I opened it upside down," said Bob, chuckling. Some people in the crowd groaned. I moved in closer as he grabbed the pile of posters and flipped them over. I gasped.

That face!

That smile!

That creep!

A huge picture of *Matthew* was staring right back at me!

"Oh, look—it's Matthew!" Grandma said,

TURKEY BURGER

$1.99

small .69
medium .19
large 2.99

at your local Burger Barn.

as if I couldn't tell. Everyone went back to their seats, disappointed, of course, but I couldn't move. Matthew's big hamburger-eating head seemed to be laughing right at me—Annie Pitts, *loser*.

Grandma put her arm around me and said, "I'm sorry you didn't win, Annie, but it's nice that one of your friends did. Matthew is going to be so surprised."

"Surprised?" I said. "He's not even here! He didn't even want his picture taken—we only brought him along because we felt sorry for him."

"Well I guess the judges liked the way he looked," Grandma said. "He *is* kind of cute, don't you think?"

I wasn't about to answer that.

Grandma took my hand and said, "Let's get a seat. We can have some dinner as long as we're here."

I said, "I don't want a hamburger." I never thought I would say those words, but out they came.

"No?" Grandma asked. She was as shocked as I was.

"It's weird," I said. "But I really don't feel like eating a hamburger. Maybe I caught something from Mercedes. Is being a vegetarian contagious?"

"I don't think so." Grandma laughed. "But we can get some pizza if you'd like."

"Extra cheese?"

"Extra cheese."

I tossed my coupons into the garbage and we headed for the Pizza 'N' Pop, my new favorite place to eat.

The next day Matthew walked into the classroom and sat at his desk, as if he were a normal person instead of a very famous poster boy. Susan congratulated him and

Thomas asked him for his autograph. Marsha didn't say anything, of course.

When everyone was seated, Miss G. made a formal announcement about Matthew's good fortune, just in case there was a single person on the planet who hadn't heard it yet. Then she told us to quietly read our chapter books while she helped some kids with their math.

Matthew opened his chapter book—just like a normal person—and started to read.

I couldn't stand it anymore. I had to say something. "Pssst," I called. He looked up.

I didn't want to sound like I was jealous or anything, so I said, "I guess you were pretty excited to hear about your poster. Did you see it hanging up, or did somebody call you?"

Matthew looked a little shy as he said, "I knew about it a couple of days ago. They sent me some posters in the mail."

"You knew? And you didn't tell anyone?" I

said loudly. Miss G. gave me a Please-Lower-Your-Voice look.

Matthew whispered back, "I don't really want my face hanging in every Burger Barn in the country. It's . . . it's embarrassing!"

It's true. Matthew was actually embarrassed. He wasn't bragging about it like Marsha-Miss-I-Win-I-Win would have done.

"You're right," I said. "It's going to be very embarrassing. People are going to draw things all over your face, you know. But congratulations anyway."

Matthew stuck his face back in his book, but I could tell that he was worried.

I guess it's not his fault that he won. He can't help it if somebody thinks he looks cute eating a hamburger. They were obviously not looking for a Little Orphan Annie type that day, so it's not my fault that I didn't win, either.

When I got home from school, I could

smell chocolate as soon as I walked in the door.

"I'm baking your favorite cake to cheer you up, Annie," Grandma said. "Double fudge chocolate chip."

"Thanks, Grandma," I said, dipping my finger into the batter. "But I'm not really upset about the contest anymore."

"No?" she asked.

"Of course not," I said. "Eating a hamburger does not require talent. I'll just wait to audition for something that does."

"Of course you will," Grandma said, and smiled. She cleared off the counter and picked up an envelope that was stuck to the bottom of the mixer.

"Oh, I almost forgot. This came for you today," she said.

I thought it might be a Christmas card from my father because he's the only one who writes to me. The postmark was from

California, but I didn't see his familiar hand-writing on the outside. I opened it and read out loud:

> *Dear* <u>Ms. Pitts,</u>
> *I thoroughly enjoyed meeting you at the* <u>Cross County Shopping Center</u> *for the Burger Barn poster contest. I'm sorry you were not one of the winners, but I'd like you to keep my card. My talent agency can always use another* <u>"Little Orphan Annie"</u> *type. Please look me up if you're ever out this way.*
> *Sincerely,*
> *Sam Schmuze*

I picked up the card that had fallen out of the envelope and onto the floor. Sure enough. It said, Super Star Talent Agency, Sam Schmuze, director.

"It's from that Sam guy who was at the

audition," I said in disbelief. "He says I should look him up if I'm ever out there."

Grandma rolled her eyes and said, "California is three thousand miles away, Annie. I don't think you'll be out there very soon."

That wasn't going to stop me. I said, "Dad lives in California, and Mom said I could fly there when I'm older. I'm older now—I'm almost ten!"

Grandma said, "That will be up to your mother, Annie. But don't go getting your hopes up again."

But my hopes were way up there. I stood in front of the bathroom mirror for the rest of the afternoon, practicing my smiles. I would practice my signature later, because I'll have to give out a lot of autographs when I become a famous person.

I was up to Smile #3, the no-teeth-showing one, when Grandma announced that the cake was ready. I stopped practicing my smiles for a cake break.

Grandma had already iced the two layers in chocolate frosting, and filled the pastry bag with creamy gold icing. I squeezed the icing through the tip and made little gold stars all around the edge. Then in the middle, I practiced my first official autograph.

I signed the cake:

Read all of the books about
Annie Pitts!

☆　☆　☆

Annie Pitts, Artichoke

"Amusing and highly palatable reading fare, with sprightly, realistically drawn illustrations that enhance the book's energy and fun."

—*Booklist*

Annie Pitts, Swamp Monster

"The slapstick humor will have young readers giggling. . . . This sequel to *Annie Pitts, Artichoke* is breezy and lighthearted."

—*School Library Journal*

Annie Pitts, Burger Kid

"Clever, humorous plot details . . . meld into a delightful, laugh-out-loud example of how the dramatic and highly imaginative Annie embellishes everyday life. . . . Fans of *Annie Pitts, Artichoke* and Annie's other adventures won't be disappointed."　　　　　—*Booklist*

2771